This ...alker book

belongs to:

_____

_____

IKE'S INCREDIBLE INK

Brianne Farley

WALKER BOOKS
AND SUBSIDIARIES
LONDON • BOSTON • SYDNEY • AUCKLAND

Ike wanted to write a story.

An incredible story.

He had read many incredible stories,
and he felt sure he could write one of his own.

He was ready to start ...

but what should he write about?

Maybe he needed to find
his favourite pen.

And have a long chat with his best friend.

And a bit of cleaning was
also in order.

But even then, something was wrong.
Something was missing.

"Hmm," said Ike.
"Maybe I need..."

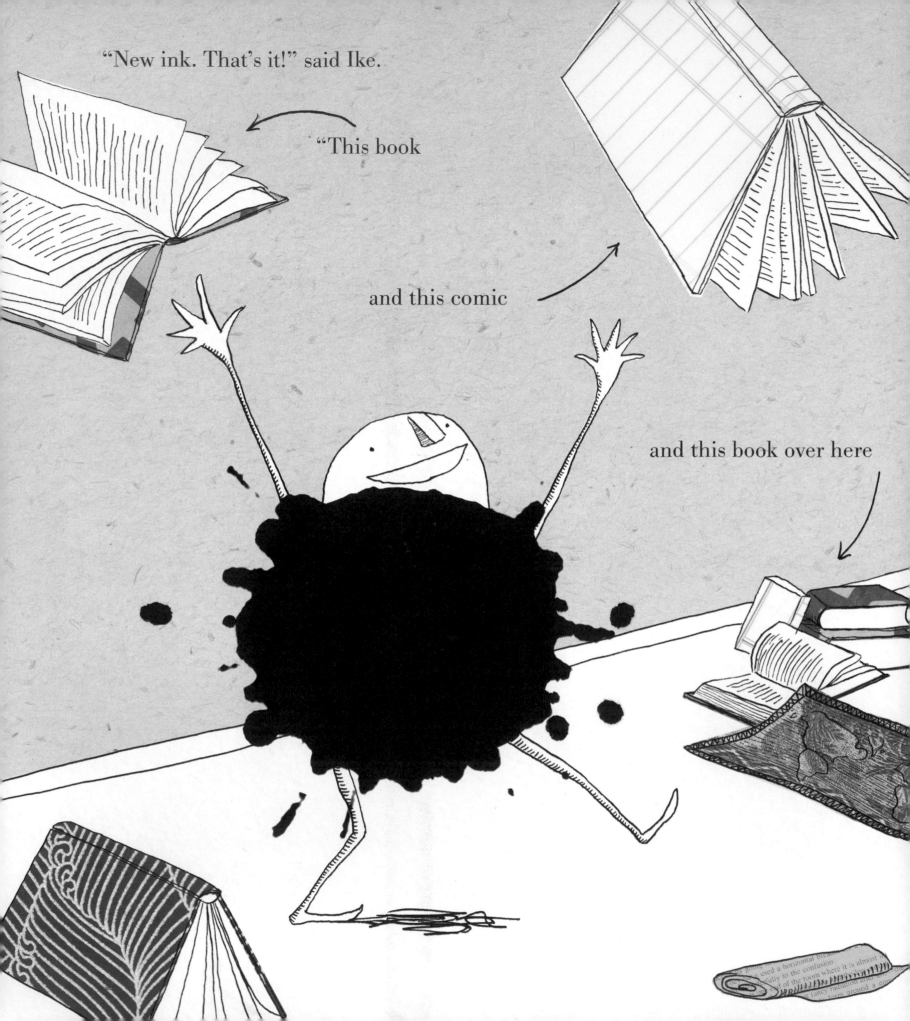

and this map

are all printed with ink. Their *very own* ink.

I need my own ink!"

"First," Ike said, "I need the right ingredients."

He looked round the room.

Shadows, he thought, *are like ink.*

They are shady and shifty and mysterious.

He shook out a shadow and put it in a big bag.

Next, Ike looked outside.
Booga-bird feathers, he thought, *are
floaty and soft like ink.*

So he gave the booga-birds their
favourite treat, took a few feathers
and stuffed them into his big bag.

Ike looked at the sky. *The dark side of the moon,* he thought, *is black like ink. It's velvety and pretty and round like a drop of ink.*

So he decided to go there.

He would, of course, need a rocket.

So he doodled and measured and lugged and planned.

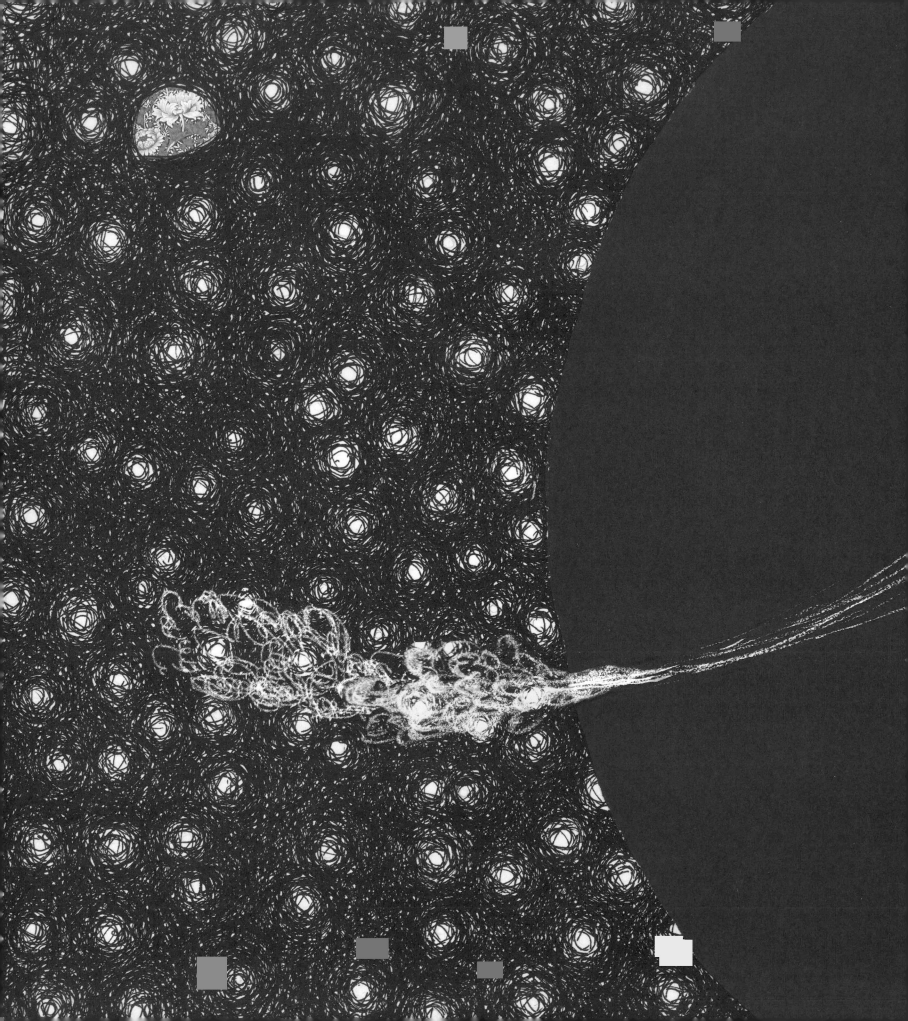

It's hard to say what Ike found on the dark side of the moon, because he didn't take a flashlight.

But whatever he found went in that big bag.

"Finally," he said, "I have everything I need."

Ike set to work.

He mashed,
he bludgeoned,
he crushed
and he steamed.

And he was definitely messy.

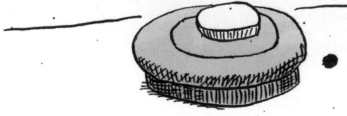

Ike bottled his ink. It looked pretty good.

He sat back down at his desk ...

HOW TO FOLD A MAP

and he started to write an incredible story.

For Mom and Dad (stargazers)
and for Allan (rocket-builder)

First published 2013 by Walker Books Ltd
87 Vauxhall Walk, London SE11 5HJ

This edition published 2014

2 4 6 8 10 9 7 5 3 1

© 2013 Brianne Farley

The right of Brianne Farley to be identified as author/illustrator
of this work has been asserted by her in accordance with
the Copyright, Designs and Patents Act 1988

This book has been typeset in Bodoni Antiqua

Printed in China

British Library Cataloguing in Publication Data:
a catalogue record for this book is available from the British Library

ISBN 978-1-4063-5549-9

www.walker.co.uk